LEATHER LUNGS
WOODEN HYDRANTS
AND EMPTY KEGS

SHAWN: YOUR FIRE DEPT. ENDEVOUR SHOULD BE ALOT MORE STRAIGHT FORWARD THAN MINE WAS. PLEASE ENJOY.

Bill

LEATHER LUNGS WOODEN HYDRANTS AND EMPTY KEGS

MY THIRTY PLUS YEARS IN THE RENSSELAER FIRE DEPARTMENT

William R. Reimann

Copyright © 2013 by William R. Reimann.

ISBN: Softcover   978-1-4931-5568-2
         Ebook   978-1-4931-5569-9

All rights reserved. No part of this book may be reproduced or transmitted in any form or by any means, electronic or mechanical, including photocopying, recording, or by any information storage and retrieval system, without permission in writing from the copyright owner.

This is a work of fiction. Names, characters, places and incidents either are the product of the author's imagination or are used fictitiously, and any resemblance to any actual persons, living or dead, events, or locales is entirely coincidental. Besides the crazy events depicted in this book could never really have happened or could they?

This book was printed in the United States of America.

Rev. date: 12/21/2013

To order additional copies of this book, contact:
Xlibris LLC
1-888-795-4274
www.Xlibris.com
Orders@Xlibris.com
141892

CONTENTS

Introduction 9

My Beginning Years 11

The Fire Alarm System 19

Some of the Characters 20

Some of the Really Big Ones 26

Jilcox Fire 30

The Knights of Columbus Fire 32

1526 Third Street 33

Fender Benders and then some 34

Starting Downhill 43

On the City's Dime 54

A DVD and Missing Things 55

1992 The Hills 100th Anniversary Celebration 57

Bazaars and Fund Raisers 60

The End 63

Exam Time 65

Dedication

This book is dedicated to my loving daughter Helena Mar (Reimann) Rambone and also to my late first wife Joann Marie Butler Reimann, for tolerating the many hours, days and years that I put into the firehouse and the Rensselaer Fire Department.

INTRODUCTION

When I decided to write this book, I was trying to come up with a good name for it.

My first idea was "My Thirty plus Years in the Rensselaer Fire Department, the Good, the Bad and the Fugly". Because there was a tremendous amount of good that happened throughout the years, there was more than its share of bad that had happened.

As far as the fugly goes, well anyone who was around during those years can attest to some of fuckin ugly things that went on in this fire department, many of which are depicted in this book.

Now for the record, the reason I chose the name for this book that I did was for a couple of reasons.

One of my favorite fire department books, of all time, is Report from Engine Company 82 that was written by Fireman Dennis Smith of the New York City Fire Department. This book was written in the late 1960's and early 1970's about a firehouse in the South Bronx, New York City during the blaze days of civil unrest. Engines 82 along with Ladder 31 during this time were answering between Eight and Nine thousand calls per year and were considered to be the busiest firehouse in the world.

One of my favorite parts in the book was a time where one of the veteran firemen of Ladder 31, a real ball buster, was berating a rookie fireman or "probie" as they are called in the firehouse kitchen. Telling him that back in his day as a "probie" they had no Scott Air Packs, (ergo leather lungs.) and had wooden hydrants. He went on to say that the probies even had to service the mares now and then. (Referring to horse drawn apparatus) I really liked this because it reminded me of my early days in the fire department.

Scott Air Packs were fairly new in the city. They were heavy, bulky, and awkward and there were just not that many to go around. Most guys were just forced to enter the fire scenes without breathing protection (Hence Leather Lungs)

Wooden hydrants, well that was because at the time of the early seventies the city's infrastructure was in pretty bad shape. This included fire hydrants, when you hit a hydrant it may or may not have water, or it may be leaking. Water was a crap shoot, and the hydrants might just as well have been made of wood.

As for the Empty Kegs, well that pretty much goes without saying for anyone who was around the firehouses of Rensselaer anytime at all in the 50's, 60's, 70's, 80's, 90's and well into the 2000's. There was simply just one hell of a lot of beer consumed, and by just about everybody. This was just the way it was back then; it was just a way of life.

Back in the day all five of the city's firehouses had bars and they were all busy for a lot of years. A lot of the city's police officers were members of the firehouses over the years and in their off duty hours made good use of the firehouse bars. Even a lot of the city's politicians were firehouse members and officers. Some of them also made good use of the bar and, in some cases, spent many overnight hours drinking beer and playing poker.

For the longest time, in the E.F.Hart Hose Firehouse, the four permanent drivers assigned there actually ran the bar, and none of them were Hart Hose members.

I really hope that anyone that reads this book takes it with a grain of salt and comes away from it with a little more of a sense of humor.

And for others I hope it brings back a lot of memories.

MY BEGINNING YEARS

I became a member of the Rensselaer Fire Department in October of 1974, when a few friends of mine and I joined the James Hill Hook and Ladder Company, Truck Number One.

Back in those days it didn't take very much to become a member of the Fire Department. All you needed was a member of the company you wished to join sponsor you and three other members of the company to co-sign your application. Then you would be voted on by the company at one of their monthly meetings using the black ball system, which today is illegal. Very few people, if any, were ever turned down for membership and the thought of a woman becoming a member was unheard of.

When I first joined the fire department, it was pretty much up to the individual as to how active you wanted to be. Training was optional and State Fire Training was just coming around. It was a fairly new concept as far as the city was concerned. Before and around this time frame, if you wanted to fight fires and you didn't happen to be at the firehouse, you would basically show up at the fire scene and hope that there would still be Turnout Gear left on the truck. Back then all the gear was carried on the truck. If you were lucky enough to find gear you would then hook up with one of the three foremen or officer in charge. At that time you pretty much learned what to do from the company officers and the senior guys.

There usually wasn't a lot of Turnout Gear to be had and what was there was old. The coats were still rubber, the helmets were cheap and you always had to search for the correct size when looking for boots. The gloves were the old cheap orange rubber like substance that were all hardened up in the shape of a claw. During those days there were a lot of members that would show up at fires and the gear was already being used. The guys would hang out at the fire scene and wait for someone who needed relief and would take over their gear, as long as it fit.

Once N.Y.S. Fire Training began to be more readily available, the more active members started taking training classes such as basics of Firemanship (Essentials), Ladder Company Operations, etc. It would take several years and even decades before this training would become mandatory in the city of Rensselaer. Each of the individual companies would have their own training and drills, such as Aerial Ladder and Ground Ladder Drills, Search and Rescue Drills etc.

One method of Search and Rescue that we did at the Hills Firehouse was one that was very basic but very effective. We would use the company meeting room and rearrange all of the furniture. We would then send two members as a team clad in full turnout gear wearing Scott Air Packs with waxed paper taped to the mask to simulate a smoke condition. They would be told to search for a small child who was supposed to be trapped in the darkened room. The small child was actually a doll that was placed in different place.

Anyway after the fires were put out and the companies had returned to quarters, the members would always help the driver on duty put the apparatus back in order.

I understand that presently at the new North End Fire Station, after the trucks have been put back in order "The firefighters", we used to be called firemen, have a special room to go to called "The BATROOM". I am not real sure what that is and am pretty sure I don't want to know. I actually have an idea or two about it but it sounds a little too much like personal satisfaction to me. Back in the day we needed to have a special room to go to after all the work was complete. It was called a Bar Room, and every firehouse had one. This was how the city rewarded the volunteer firemen for all of their time and effort.

This process lasted for many decades until the insurance liability became too great to serve alcohol in the city owned firehouses. But it sure was a great thing while it lasted.

After a fire, the guys would hang around the "Bar Room" for an hour or two and drink beer paid for by the company via the Foreman's Fund. The foreman and two assistants were the forerunners of the current fire officers. It was a great time to be involved with the fire department in the mid 1970's and into the 1980's. The volunteers and the paid drivers all pretty much got along and everyone did their jobs and the fires always were put out. There were a lot of them.

Around that time there began to be an alarming influx of arson fires in the city.

I don't think that these younger guys around today could possibly grasp what it was like during that time period. Today whenever there is a structure fire it's treated like a huge event. But back then it just seemed like business as usual. Sometimes there would be several two or three alarm fires a week and sometimes there would even be more than one fire going on at once.

I can remember fighting a fire at the corner of Second Street and Fowler Avenue and looking down at another structure fire going at the corner of First Street and Fowler Avenue. (Fowler Avenue at that time still ran all the way from Broadway to Fifth Street.)

These arson fires would go on like this for several more years until two of these suspected arsonists would meet their deaths.

One of them died in a fire that he himself set in the Fifteen Hundred block of Second Street. It would be a week before his body was recovered because no one knew he was in there and the building had collapsed. It was only after he had gone missing after that fire that it was suspected that he may be in there. I fought that fire and can remember the smell of a strange odor in the air that night.

The other individual suspected in these fires wound up dying in a drowning incident if I can remember correctly. Right after the demise of these two arson suspects the fires dramatically decreased.

Aside from the death of this one arsonist by his own hand, there were never any serious injuries from all these fires, despite the fact that some of these buildings had been lit up sometimes two, three or four times before the city got around to tearing them down.

People forget the vast loss of property that took up most of the area that ran between McNaughton Avenue and Central Avenue, and Broadway and Upper Second Street. There are still quite a few of the original homes remaining in this area. But the rest of it is either vacant lots or what is now known as the Turnkey Housing Project. These were all at one time neighborhoods and almost all of it was taken by fire, intentionally set.

Some years later there would be another person who began starting fires in the city because he was having a beef with a city police officer. What this individual would do is to set fires next to or near relatives of this police officer to try and intimidate him.

I was a victim of these fires twice because of my wife's relation to the officer. Fortunately, these fires never amounted to much and after several months of very close calls the police department set up a sting operation and the arsonist was arrested, tried and found guilty. He was sent to prison where he died just a few years ago.

Other wild times around those days were on Election Night. This is another example of when you tell these younger firefighters of today as to how many calls and how many fires there were, they just wouldn't believe it. Some election nights there were as many as fifty to close to one hundred calls between six o'clock at night until midnight. Most of these fires were bonfires, but they were spread out all through the city. Some of these fires grew very large and were at regular locations.

First and John Street along with Partition and Fifth Street were popular locations just to name a few. These bon fires began to start having a following and even appeared to be something of a competition. As soon as the companies would put out these fires and go off to the next call, the vandals who would always have more fuel stashed away, hidden in sheds, alleyways etc. They would have another fire roaring in no time flat.

It was crazy to watch; as the pumpers would respond from bonfire to bonfire, there would be a line of cars parading behind the apparatus, sometimes fifteen to twenty cars. It used to get so busy at times that Pumper One from the city's lower end would wind up in Eastland Park in the city's northern end. Pumper Four from the North End would wind up in the city's lower end.

Eventually over the years the bon fires graduated into more serious vacant structure fires and things slowly started getting out of hand. Between the arson fires of the mid 1970's and all those election nights there was a lot of on the job training for a lot of people.

Another thing that we had a lot of back then were false alarms and there were a lot of them. Two or three of them a night was normal with up to five or six if some kid felt inspired. False alarms are now pretty much a thing of the past with maybe just a few per year.

The fire department since its beginning had been using American LaFrance as its choice for fire apparatus. Now a lot of people thought that these trucks were junk. But some of these trucks served the city for up to thirty years under terrible conditions and with very little preventive maintenance.

For example, Pumper 3, a 1961 American LaFrance 900 series Open Cab Pumper remained in front line service until the early 1990's, despite low maintenance and surviving two major accidents. Her sister truck, Pumper I, was in service just about as long with all but her last few years still using a gasoline engine. To me these two pieces of apparatus along with Pumper 2, a 1967 American LaFrance 900 series, which over its lifetime responded to hundreds of off road calls such as brush fires, bon fires etc. Additionally, Truck 1, a 1968 American LaFrance 900 series Aerial Ladder, that itself survived a major accident.

These vehicles were a testament to quality of American workmanship and very few municipalities could lay claim to the length of service and the amount of use that these trucks endured.

Ironically Pumper 4, the newest of all trucks at the time, a 1974 American LaFrance 1000 series. Pumper 4 lasted the least amount of years. These trucks were knocked down, dragged out, picked up and rung out like an old wash cloth but kept on going and going.

My brother and I wound up owning the Pumper 3 truck with the intention of restoring her but found that we had to sell her because of lack of storage space. At this time, the truck with its 671 Detroit Diesel Engine ran as strong as the day city mechanic Ernie Haymew installed it back in the early 1970's.

You may have noticed that I refer to these trucks as Pumpers and not engines. That's because these trucks don't engine water, they pump water, and ergo they are pumpers.

All of the afore mentioned apparatus with the exception of Pumper 4 had no power steering and all of them had standard transmissions. They were not at all that pleasant to drive. A lot of guys came on the job over the years and some came on with little or no truck driving experience. These trucks all took a certain amount of abuse while many of these guys learned how to drive and operate them. This was just another example of how hard these vehicles were beaten down and just kept coming on back for more.

Another ironic thing of how things go in this city, is back in the days of the mid 1970's thru the mid 1980's is the equipment we had was old and outdated. But still we fought all of those fires without ever giving it a second thought. In today's fire department, the apparatus is very modern and the turnout gear and equipment is much more high tech.

And even though the fire department responds to a lot more calls per year now than it did back then, today there are very few fires (which is not a bad thing). Most of the calls today are medical in nature. The truth is, with the exception of a select few, almost everyone involved with today's fire department will never in their lifetime see the amount of fires that we fought back then. And I hope for everyone's sake they never will.

It wasn't always serious business. There were a lot of good times in the fire department. Parties, Installation Dinners, Parties, Parades, Parties, Picnics, Parties and Friendly Rivalries between the other companies like softball games played for half kegs of beer. And, oh, did I mention all the Parties?

One of the craziest things that went on at the Hills Firehouse was the Annual Spring Jug Party. This was really nothing more than a glorified clam bake. This party drew a lot of members every year and besides all the great food and beer, the afternoon was capped off with a baseball dart game which was held on the apparatus floor. The driver on duty that day would pull the truck outside for the day and we would pretty much take over the firehouse.

Two teams were made up as the old timers against the youngsters, Varsity vs. JV. It was, to put it mildly, loud, and noisy beyond belief. There was yelling, screaming, throwing of folding metal chairs and smashing trash cans, anything that would distract the dart thrower. We would drink beer, eat and smoke on the apparatus floor and just raise hell all afternoon. Never once was there an issue. I wonder how the drivers of today would have handled that.

The firehouses themselves had a lot of rich history going back to the mid to late 1800's.

In 1992, the James Hill Hook and Ladder Co. celebrated its 100th Anniversary. And that same year, the J.N. Ring Co. Pumper One celebrated its 150th Anniversary, while just a few years before the E.F. Hart Hose had celebrated their 100th Anniversary.

The G.S. Mink and T. Claxton Hose Company Pumper 2 Firehouse also goes back a long way. The original firehouse once stood just to the south of the current one at the very foot of John Street and Broadway. It also housed City Hall and the Police Department.

The J.N. Ring Firehouse on Second Avenue in the city's lower end was my favorite as far as the building itself. It was quite a remarkable structure that had also housed the Police Department at one time. There were still jail cells on the first floor. The building had many different levels and rooms at every turn. When I was a relief driver in the late eighties and early nineties I used to love working out of that building.

The E.F. Hart Hose Firehouse on East Street and Herrick Street with the diaphone air horn mounted on the roof was quite an experience to work out of. When a box alarm was received you could feel and hear the whoosh of air coming from the compressor going up to the roof to sound the horn. This was something else when an alarm would come in the middle of the night while you were in a dead sleep. It got your attention.

Back in those days, unlike now, there were usually a lot of guys hanging around the firehouses, especially on Friday and Saturday Night. Whether it is hanging at the bars, playing cards or maybe just hanging out on the apparatus floor with the driver.

When an alarm would come in almost everyone would jump on the trucks. It must have been quite a sight to see for ordinary people. It wasn't unusual to have eight to ten guys hanging all over the truck grabbing onto whatever they could. And remember the pumpers back then actually still had back steps on them. Imagine that.

A lot of guys came up from the bar area and drunk or sober off they went. What the hell, depending on what firehouse you were in the driver on duty had probably knocked back more than a few. It's truly amazing that no one was ever hurt much less killed. But that's really just the way things were back then and nobody even batted an eye.

Just to add a bit more chaos to it, for many years at the Hart Hose Firehouse they had a Dalmatian named Mandy that actually lived at the firehouse fulltime and was cared for by the drivers. Mandy not only lived at the firehouse but she would actually ride the truck to calls. Whenever the bell hit or the fire phone rang Mandy would jump right up onto the truck. The biggest downside to this was Mandy barked a lot and slobbered a lot. It could be a little messy.

When I first joined the fire department the ranks of the paid drivers were still fully staffed at twenty five men and would remain that way for a few more years. In those years there were still five fire houses in service. Pumper 4 would be closed around 1988.

There were four men permanently assigned to each of the five firehouses, one each on the A, B, C and D shift. Four more permanent drivers would each be assigned a shift (A, B, C, or D shift). These men would cover sick days, vacation days and when they were not needed; they would work as second man at the Hills Firehouse on their assigned shift. The twenty-fifth man was assigned the Kelley shift and worked the other drivers extra day off. This was all a great system; the drivers could get the apparatus to the emergency scenes very quickly. They would drive and operate the apparatus and the volunteers would do the hose work, the ladder work and the rescue work. I guess it must have worked to good.

So a few years down the road when the city started talking about budget, cuts the local politicians can't help but start meddling in the fire department. The fire departments of most cities always seem to be the traditional whipping boys.

The mayor at the time was Joseph Finke and he seemed to be following the lead of his friend, then Cohoes Mayor Ron Canacook, who at the time was meddling with his own fire department.

Mayor Finke wanted to close the Hart Hose Fire house. But to the mayors surprise he met up with some stiff opposition because of a strong campaign by both the Drivers' Union with assistance from the volunteers. The mayor's plan was doomed, for now, but it would be just a precursor of the times to come later on.

The city began downsizing the paid department over the years first by attrition

But then in the early 1990's there had been some bad blood going on between the Drivers' Union and Mayor Joseph Corrigan. The mayor was putting on a strong campaign to drastically cut the ranks of the paid drivers. The city eventually offered a retirement incentive on pretty much a take it or leave it basis to the most senior drivers. Most took the deal but the city did wind up laying off two drivers with least seniority. These two men would later be brought back about a year later.

The department had been brought down to twelve paid men and had started using part time relief drivers some years earlier, at first only for vacation days and later for extended sick days also. During the time of all this turmoil and talks of budget cuts and layoffs, no other departments in the city ever had the threat of layoffs looming over their heads.

The whole thing was clearly a personal vendetta because of the issues Mayor Horrigan was having with the drivers' union.

In my opinion the fire department was the best thing the city had to offer. With the paid drivers and volunteer fireman it always seemed like the perfect balance.

THE FIRE ALARM SYSTEM

The way the alarm system was set up made response time in the city second to none for both Fire Calls and E.M.S . . . At the time, with the fire phone system, the men that answered the emergency fire phone were also the very men who would be responding to the call. The emergency fire phone was some set up. It was an old fashioned dial type phone, only without the dial. It was for incoming calls only.

These phones were located in each of the five firehouses and they were located throughout the firehouses on every floor, (even in the bars) so no driver would ever be very far from one. There was also one located at the Police Stations Front Desk.

When a call came in the driver stationed at the Hills Firehouse would let the phone ring about seven times to give everyone else time to get to one of the phones, then he would answer it. The other four drivers and the police dispatcher would listen. After determining the nature of the call the Hills driver would dispatch the proper apparatus.

If the call was for a structure fire the Hills driver would tell the police dispatcher to transmit the nearest box number. With the ladder truck and two pumpers responding, answering the fire phone would now fall to one of the remaining pumper drivers. In a case where all the companies were out of quarters the police dispatcher would then take over.

This system was very old, antiquated and required a lot of maintenance but it worked very well for decades.

Try to remember that back then was well before the age of cell phones and pagers. So with the bells and horns tapping out the box numbers, as long as you had an alarm card and you could count, you knew where the fire was.

SOME OF THE CHARACTERS

Like most fire departments and or fire houses. There is always the never ending ball busting and practical jokes being played on one another. If you have thin skin you'd be better off to stay home, in other words if you can't run with the big dogs then stay on the porch.

There was always a never ending supply of Looney characters that had something to do with the Rensselaer Fire Department, in one way or another. Some were stranger than others. These people ran the whole gamut, from fire drivers to volunteers. So I am going to begin with probably the wackiest individual of all time.

One of the drivers that I worked with over the years both as a relief driver and a volunteer was Doug "The Bug" Cucumber. That pretty much says it all there. Doug worked on the fire department for about twenty five years and was one crazy character.

I'll start with one of the wildest stories about him.

One weekend afternoon there was the usual crowd hanging out at the bar of the Hills Firehouse. One of the people at the bar that day was the driver on duty Frank Welsh. Now it had been long rumored that Frank had quietly been seeing the same woman that Doug had been dating and Doug had apparently gotten wind of it. So at some point Doug decided that he was going to confront Frank about this debacle.

Well I guess Doug walks onto the apparatus floor and back towards the kitchen, no Frank. So now he goes upstairs to the driver's bedroom, still no Frank. Next stop was to the bar, so Doug walks down the stairs from the apparatus floor and spots Frank sitting at the bar.

So Doug approaches Frank and low and behold he's got a handgun. He promptly shoves the gun right in Frank's face and says he's going to kill him if he doesn't stop seeing his girl. Now while Frank is about shittin in his pants, John Steelhead who was behind the bar pouring beer starts shouting "Shoot Him, Shoot Him, Shoot Him. If you run out of bullets my gun is right over there on the table".

Now John was a funny little guy that stood about four feet nothing and had a broad mustache that made him look a lot like Yosemite Sam from the Bugs Bunny cartoons. By this time the rest of the guys had wrestled the gun away from Doug and things were calming down. And in true Rensselaer fashion the police were never called that day but at some point both men had to have a little sit down with then Police Chief Charlie Slewerd.

Bub Grunt one of the Hill Hooks longtime members whose been hanging out at the firehouses for decades. Over the years Bub took a lot of heat from Doug "The Bug," but Bub always found a way to get his revenge.

When Doug worked he would send Bub down to Chet's corner store and have him pick up candy bars and ice cream, and upon returning to the firehouse Bub loved to leave them on the apparatus floors baseboard heaters. Doug's nickname "Doug the Bug" was a very fitting name because he truly was a ten card carrying bed bug.

He was a career college student who majored in nothing and when he wasn't working in the firehouse we all really thought that he lived in his car. He was also afraid of the dark. He would sleep all day and was up all night. He was very paranoid and it was rumored that he kept a rope ladder in the driver's bedroom in case of a fire. When he was working he would come down to the bar late at night and have a few beers.

Doug was a germafobe and everything had to be very clean, even though he looked and dressed like a bum. His shirt was always untucked, his pants were always falling down over his ass and his hair was never combed. So he would come down stairs and walk up to the bar, ask the bartender for a clean glass. Then go into the bathroom and clean the glass himself. Then he would come out of the bathroom shaking the water drops off the glass over each shoulder.

When he referred to other people he would give them names such as Joe Balls, Pete Bumfuck or Jimmie Gozolini. One day Doug was in the drivers kitchen with Bub Grunt and he looked out the window down towards the little league field and noticed two squirrels running around.

So Doug decides to open the window and toss a doughnut to them but they ignore it. Doug says to Bub, look, look, look at that, a dumb Rensselaer Squirrel. And he starts yelling out the window "Hey dumb Rensselaer Squirrel eat the doughnut" and, of course, they still ignore him. Doug makes up a sign that says "Dumb Rensselaer Squirrel please eat the doughnut". Then he sends Bub Grunt down behind the firehouse and Bub tacks the sign to a nearby tree.

Another time when Doug was still working on the B-shift and Roger Dunst was working down in the Rings Firehouse. Now Roger was one of those guys who would take full advantage of the bar while on duty, if ya know what I mean. So a call comes in for the lower end for a brush fire or something like that and Doug sends the Rings with Roger at the wheel.

Now back at this time the fire department was still working off one of the county radio frequencies. Pumper One was E-37, Pumper 2 was E-38, Pumper 3 was E-39, Pumper 4 was E-40 and Truck One was L-29.

After Roger had arrived on the scene and went to report back to L-29 he started calling on the radio, E-37 to E-37. Meanwhile back at the truck house Doug along with Bub Grunt says, did, did ya hear that, he's, he's calling himself. And Doug says "Let's let him go for a little while". Sure enough after a minute or so, E-37 calling E-37, finally Doug says to Roger "What do you want Roger, your calling yourself?"

One boring night while I was working at the Hills Firehouse, I was sitting in the kitchen looking thru some of the old log books. There were always some funny entries in them from time to time and I eventually came across one that Doug had written at one time. He'd had a call for a smoke detector going off at the Gerald O'Neil American L Legion Post on Broadway.

After having the box was transmitted and the units arrived, it soon was discovered that the source of the smoke was from one of the party goer's pipe. It turned out the pipe smoker was one of our own members from the Hills named Dan Boomhower. Now this is funny because Dan had a reputation of when he smoked his pipe the smoke could fill a room or even block out the sun, and it smelled bad, real bad.

So upon returning to quarters Doug writes in the log book. Received call on fire phone for smoke detector going off at the O'Neil Post, Box 122 transmitted. Smoke detector was set off by Dan Boomhowers Pipe. This was one of the many things that Dan never lived down.

Doug could be just as cold hearted as he was crazy and funny. One morning I had just gone on duty working the A-shift at pumper 3 and Doug was working at the Hills.

Just before radio check I get a call on the house phone and it's Doug. And he says well its official, its official Easty's dead, Easty's dead.

Easty was James East, a retired fire driver and recently retired fire chief. He was also a very popular and active person in the city for most of his life. I had just found out that he had die earlier that morning from an apparent heart attack.

So Doug continues to rant on "Well I don't know what I am gonna do now, he owed me a day, maybe I can get it back from Gert (Jims wife)". Man he could be cold.

Back when there were still two drivers assigned to the Hills Firehouse, Gary VanVooster had the dubious pleasure of being assigned to the B-shift with Doug. It was bad luck all around for Gary. But he quickly learned to make the best of it with practical joke. Here's an example of one of his best.

Because Doug would sleep all day it gave Gary plenty of time to plot out his fun.

Gary would love to take Doug's canned goods and switch the labels around on them. I am pretty sure that he had done this on more than one occasion. I think maybe once or twice he may even have switched dog food for his corned beef hash. Now that's funny shit. One day when Gary and Doug were working together a call came in while Doug was in the apparatus floor kitchen.

Gary was upstairs in the driver's bunkroom, probably taking his daily constitutional. Doug being the crazy nervous maniac he was just jumped in the truck leaving Gary behind in the dust. Gary to say the least was not a happy camper, but Chris Yonkos who had been downstairs at the bar came upstairs to find out what was going on.

So Chris after speaking with an irate Gary drives him to the call in his personal vehicle, where Gary promptly reamed Doug a new asshole. Needless to say Doug never did that again.

One character from the Hills Firehouse was a person I never actually met, because he had moved to Florida just before I became a member. His name was Charlie Pohl and over the years I had heard many, many stories about him. From what I've heard about him I think he was someone I would have gotten along very well with.

Charlie and his wife lived in the building right next door to the fire house in the upstairs apartment over what would later become Jims Pizza. Charlie was a glazer and every day, like clockwork, when he came home he would throw his work gear inside the vestibule for his apartment and make his way over to the firehouse bar. Charlie would sit in the same bar stool day after day and was a real creature of habit. Charlie loved his beer and it's said that when he moved away the firehouse bar had to order one less half of beer per week.

Every night around dinner time Charlie would call next door and ask his wife what she was making for dinner. Her response would always be, I 'am makin shit, and with that Charlie without blinking an eye, would tell her make enough for one I won't be home.

Another guy who you also set your watch by was "Big Joe" Forceful. Big Joe was a firehouse regular, seven days a week, no matter what. Joe worked in downtown Albany and got out of work at Five o'clock sharp and was usually at the firehouse bar by Five-O-Five sharp. One of the first things Joe would come out with every night when he arrived would be what time he expected the sun to set every night.

Joe was a very active member in his younger years and in his later years he never stopped his constant barrage of entertaining wisdom. Joe was for most of his life a true beer lover but later on switched to scotch and became quite a student on that subject. When Joe went from beer to scotch sometime in the late seventies or early eighties this was another time when the firehouse bar had to order one less half of beer a week. Joe passed away in the early 2000's as the James Hill Hook and Ladders oldest members and, in many ways, one of its most colorful.

Another of the Hill Hooks eldest members is Chris Yonkos. He is one of the very few men who did more for the James Hill Hook and Ladder than most others. Chris is of one the members that has been around for over fifty years and has been active for all of this time, which is unusual.

Besides being a fire driver for twenty five years and retiring in 1992, Chris has been in charge of running some of the largest company events in its history. Most notably being the "General Chairman of the company's "One Hundredth Anniversary".

Chris made his greatest gift to the firehouse when in the 1960's he started the "Bar Room" as most of us knew it. Chris and I quickly became friends when I joined the firehouse and we worked together over the years on dozens of projects. I was honored to be handpicked by him to be his successor as bar chairman when he decided to give it up in 1992 after twenty five years. I had had nothing but respect for Chris since my day one in the fire department; he in some ways has been my mentor in the fire department.

My first ride on a call was with him as the driver. When I first became a relief driver my first day was in the Hart Hose and he dispatched me on my first call.

But back to the bar, it was always his pride and joy, even after he retired and gave up the bar.

Chris, after all of this and retiring, had many good years of enjoyment at the bar with parties, celebrations or just hanging out with fellow members on a Saturday or Sunday afternoon including many, many super Sundays over dozens of years. Of course many of these super Sunday parties were put on by Chris himself.

To this day even though I rarely see anyone much anymore, I still count Chris as one of my very best friends.

Chris and the Yonkos family have a very long history in the Rensselaer Fire Department. Chris's father John Yonkos was a paid driver at the James Hill Hook and Ladder Company dating back to the horse drawn rigs. In our 100th Anniversary book there is a picture of John Yonkos Sr. behind the wheel of the 1915 Mack truck chassis with the 1908 ladder wagon that had been retro fitted to it.

Chris used to tell some very interesting stories about his father and his days on the job. One story he loved to tell was that his father worked a Six day, 24 hour per day shift, Monday thru Saturday. On the seventh day, his relief who was a drunk wouldn't show up most of the time.

Another story would be about the firehouse horses. Just, as today, with the paid on duty drivers being in charge of the daily upkeep and maintenance of the apparatus, it was also the onus of the drivers of the early 1900's to take care of the horses in each firehouse. Feeding and training of these animals (and by training I mean teaching them to line up under the harnesses hanging overhead from the apparatus floor ceilings. And of course the drivers were responsible for cleaning out the stalls, in other words shovel the shit.)

According to Chris, some fire houses would take better care of their horses than other firehouses. For instance the Hills drivers would take better care of their horses than the driver did at the Minks.

If an alarm would come in for the North End of Broadway and the Hills Company and the Minks Company left quarters at the same time, the horse team from the Hills would eventually catch up with and overtake the Minks team somewhere around McNaughton Avenue or so.

Can you imagine what a sight it must have been to see these two fire companies racing up Broadway side by side for a few blocks at a full gallop responding to an alarm?

That really had to be something to see.

SOME OF THE REALLY BIG ONES

One of the largest fires that we had back in the mid to late 1970's was the Teals Bowling Alley Fire at the very west end of Second Avenue. The call came in sometime around midnight and there was a small group of us at the bar. We had just returned from a mattress fire at Broadway and McNaughton Avenue. It took a few minutes longer to arrive at the scene because the Broadway viaduct was closed at the time for replacement. We had to respond by way of East Street to Adams Street and over the Third Avenue Bridge.

Upon arrival there was a lot of smoke and heat but no visible fire. Frank Welsh was the driver on duty that night and had the Aerial Ladder up and placed on the roof. Along with myself were Foreman Dave Raid, Asst. Foreman Joe Bowler and Dan Boomhower. We were all bunched up on the turntable preparing to go up and vent the roof. Right about that time someone from one of the pumper companies broke out one of the front windows and that's when all hell broke loose.

Apparently the fire had been burning and smoldering since shortly after closing time earlier that night and was starved for oxygen. With the rush of fresh air the entire building exploded. Everyone except Frank Welsh and I were blown right off the turntable and anyone near the front of the building were blown right off their feet. Fortunately there were no serious injuries but the building or what was left of it was now a roaring inferno.

For what seemed like an eternity there was an eerie silence while everyone gained their composure. One thing I can remember was the voice of Doug Cucumber who had appeared out of nowhere and had jumped into one of the trucks and was yelling over the radio, "Mayday, Mayday Fire at the Bowling Alley". This fire would burn all night and well into the next day before it was brought under control. I remember when daylight came the next morning I was at the top of the Aerial Ladder using the ladder pipe and looking down into the shell of the building and seeing the large steel I-beams that once supported the roof lying there looking like pretzel twists.

Another memorable fire that occurred around this time frame was on Columbia Street at Washington Street. This was the first fire I was at where there was a fatality. I think the driver on duty that night was again Frank Welsh, but I am not sure. Among others from the Hill Hooks were Foreman Dave Raid, Asst. Foreman Joe Bowler, Bob Waiter and myself. Bob and I were working together on the roof near the front of the building ventilating this large three story apartment building.

Joe Bowler comes up the Aerial Ladder and onto the roof. Joe had just found out that an African American man had been found dead in the fire. Now Joe usually was not one to mince words and could be considered somewhat racist. But this time he quietly comes up to Bob and me and calmly says "I think a colored fella just died". Bob and I just looked at each other and exploded in laughter and Bob says to Joe "If that guy had one last dying breath left in him he'd be a no good fuckin nigger, but now he's dead and he's a colored fella".

Now we were all located on the roof at the front of the building near the tip of the Aerial Ladder. What we didn't know was that the intercom system on the Aerial Ladder was turned on, and with Dave Raid and the driver back down on the turntable, this whole thing was blared out all over the street. Fortunately, there were no friends or relatives of the deceased anywhere nearby.

As I mentioned earlier, there were times when we had a lot of fires over a short period of time. The next was a double fatality fire over Fedelee's Store at Second and Pine Streets. Two children perished in this fire. A few of us had been hanging around the firehouse on the apparatus floor with the driver on duty Jim East. A call came in on the fire phone around eight o'clock for a heavy smoke condition at Second and Pine. The first of two mistakes were made here. East should have had a box transmitted but instead dispatched Pumper Four, which was the second mistake. Pumper Two was much closer.

I'll never forget when Pumper Four arrived at the scene with Driver Frank screaming over the radio that the building was fully involved. By the time a box was transmitted and Truck One and Pumper Two arrived on the scene the building was a raging inferno. Despite the best efforts of everyone, two children perished in this fire because they were left alone by their babysitter. The fact that a box should have been transmitted from the start probably would have had little effect on the outcome of this fire, it just had too good of a start.

Moving back down to the city's lower end, there was a large fire that probably could have been kept to a minimum. On the corner of Second Avenue and Walker Street once stood Ryan's Starry Plough, a very popular watering hole around this time. This bar was located right across from the J.N. Ring Firehouse on Walker Street.

Fire Driver Charlie Fink was the On-Duty driver that night when rumor has it that one of the bar patrons ran over to the firehouse to report a fire in the kitchen at Ryan's. And the story goes, instead of calling the fire into the other companies, Chuck decided to walk over and have a look for himself. By the time Chuck located the fire, went back to the fire house, reported the fire and got the pumper out and hooked up, the fire was out of control. Needless to say the building was a total loss, and what was left had to be torn down. To make matters worse, the owners did not have up-to-date insurance coverage, so they truly lost everything. The empty lot is there till this day. Chuck was basically a good guy, but very cocky and pretty full of himself.

One day Jim Hoagerty was working in the Hills Firehouse and Chuck was working in the Rings. He calls Jim on the house phone and Jim answers Rensselaer Truck One. Chuck on the other end says "Hey, what's up kiddo". So Jim hangs up the phone. A minute later, the house phone rings again in the Hills and Jim answers Rensselaer truck one. Chuck on the other end says "Hey Sonny what's goin on? Again Jim hangs up. Another minute later, the phone rings again at the Hills. Jim answers Rensselaer Truck One and Chuck says "Hey Hoags what's goin on? You keep hangin up on me." So Jim says well there's no kiddo here and there's no Sonny here so I figured they were wrong numbers.

Another time, early on in Chuck's career, while working at the Hills, Chuck was down stairs at the bar pestering some of the members as only he could. After a while some of the guys had had enough, most of all Joe Forceful, easily the largest member of the firehouse and fondly called "Big Joe" or "The Moose." Joe calmly turns around and with one hand grabs Chuck by the balls and his other hand on Chuck's shirt collar. Then he proceeded to hoist him up over his head and pressed him up against the basement ceiling like a set of dumb bells. Well Chuck quickly cried "Uncle" and the moose set him down. That gave Chuck a little attitude adjustment for a while.

Another fatal fire we had back circa mid 1980's to late 1980's. This fire occurred in the Eight Hundred block of Third Street just south of Harrison Avenue around Three o'clock on a Saturday afternoon.

As usual there was a somewhat large group of us hanging out at the bar when we heard someone walk down the stairs from the apparatus floor and there was a knock at the door. We thought nothing of this because it was something that Bub Grunt would do all the time so we just blew it off and ignored it. That door was never locked at the time and usually Bub would just walk in after a few minutes. But then we hear the footsteps go back up the stairs. A minute later the bell hits and the guys start running up the stairs to jump on the truck.

I went out the side door to grab my personal gear from my pickup. Once outside I see Tony Katugna from the pizza shop next door running down to tell us about the fire just up the street. We all jump on the truck and off we go with Doug Cucumber at the wheel.

Upon arrival, we have a structure fire going with heavy smoke and fire at the rear of the building. We also have a man lying on the sidewalk in front of the building and his hair is burned off his head, face and arms. There had apparently been some kind of propane or natural gas explosion at the rear of the building. After rending first aid, as best we could, the Rensselaer Ambulance was on the scene quickly and transported the burn victim to the hospital, where he later died.

We had now turned our attention to the fire. The rear of the building was completely ablaze and with a very strong west wind fanning the flames, I have never seen a fire move so fast through a building like this before, from west to east this building was destroyed in what seemed like a matter of minutes. The building next door to the south was also destroyed, and the biggest problem there was the gas service had been interrupted and needed to be shut down A.S.A.P. It eventually was and several hours later the fire was under control.

It was a wild afternoon, as it turned out it was a woman knocking on the door downstairs at the firehouse bar that afternoon. Apparently she had entered the firehouse via the apparatus floor, gone to the kitchen, no one there, then yelled upstairs, no answer. Remember what I had said about Doug sleeping all day. So she went downstairs and knocked on the door, no answer. With no response she simply left.

JILCOX FIRE

The fire at the Jilcox Household was around the mid 1980's while I was still living at 1238 Second Street. I heard a call come over the scanner for a chimney fire at 1237 Second Street. This was directly across the street from my house. I knew my neighbor had a fireplace in their living room. They were having some work done on his house and there was scaffolding on the side of the house that went around the chimney.

I looked out my front door and didn't see anything showing. As I went to my truck and put my gear on Pumper Two, Pumper Four and the Ladder Truck were all arriving. Chief East had arrived on the scene. He and a handful of guys went inside the house trying to determine exactly what the fire condition was.

While all of this was going on one of the members of the Hills, Dick Whitless had decided on his own to climb up the scaffolding carrying a dry chemical fire extinguisher. Now Dick's nickname was "Whoopie Pickle" which pretty much says it all. No one knew that Dick was doing this. Dick finally makes his way to the top of the scaffolding and decides to empty the entire contents of the dry chemical extinguisher down the chimney.

The chemical powder hit the bottom of the fireplace and just blew out into the whole room and pretty much throughout the entire house. Everybody and everything inside the house were totally covered in white powder.

I'll never forget the chief, who was a big man, coming out of the house and onto the front porch. He was covered from head to toe and, in his turnout gear; he looked like the biggest, and most pissed off Pillsbury Doughboy that there ever was! On Dick's part, it was a completely boneheaded thing to do, and the chief was beyond livid. Whatever fire there had been in the fireplace or the chimney was, of course, extinguished. And holy shit what a mess the inside of that house was.

When all was said and done, the city wound up paying for the cleanup and damages. What an embarrassment for the fire department.

I was the foreman at this time and any time after that incident, whenever I saw my across the street neighbor I always wondered what he was thinking.

THE KNIGHTS OF COLUMBUS FIRE

This fire was one of the big ones that I missed in the late seventies. It was the Knights of Columbus building on the corner of Washington Avenue and Manor Drive. This fire occurred on a weekend when I was away at the Brant Lake getaway. This one hit a little close to home. My parents' house was right across Manor Drive from the side door of the K of C. And I was still living there at the time.

It was a very large fire that did extensive damage throughout the entire building and had started sometime in the late evening. The fire was an all-night event. All five companies from the city were committed to this fire with mutual aid coming in from surrounding communities to cover the city.

Incredibly, with all the noise and commotion and despite my parents' bedroom facing the K of C and their windows being open, my father managed to sleep through the entire event.

For the record, back at the time of this fire, the K of C was still being operated by the old regime. Despite the heavy damage throughout the building, the membership was able to rehab and remodel the structure to a "State of the Art Club" of the time.

If this incident had occurred twenty or so years later, when the old timers were mostly gone, the place more than likely would have folded. And it did eventually fall apart twenty to thirty years later due to mismanagement and pilfering by the membership.

After all of those great years of putting on terrific parties, wonderful banquets and numerous wedding receptions, the Knights of Columbus is now located at the former Seven Sons Restaurant at the ass end of East Street.

1526 THIRD STREET

Another one of the larger fires that occurred in the early ninety's literally hit very close to home.

This fire was a raging inferno when the companies arrived and it was right next door to where I had been living at the time.

Ironically, I should have been working at Pumper Four had it not been for a late schedule change by Chief Alboring. It was the school's spring recess and I was not scheduled to work in either the Fire Department or School District. I was spending the time at our Brant Lake Camp with my wife and daughter.

At around 11:00 p.m. on the night of the fire we received a phone call from my brother in law Bob Waiter, who was at the time a Rensselaer Police Officer. He was calling us to tell us about the fire next door and let us that there was a good chance, at that point, that we may lose our house.

There was about thirty feet separating the two houses and the fire was out of control at that time. It never got to the point of losing the house but the fire got so hot that it damaged the siding of our house, cracked some window panes and was hot enough to melt parts of the rubber roof to the point that several firemen on the roof left boot prints in it. The fire also did damage to one of my vehicles parked in my driveway, to the Vinyl Roof and melted some lenses. My garage door had some cracked window panes.

Needless to say despite the best efforts of the fire department the house at 1526 third was a total loss.

This fire was one of the very few I missed.

FENDER BENDERS AND THEN SOME

There have been several mishaps, over the years, with the various fire apparatus over the years.

Most were minor accidents. Others were rather large events, involving not only fire apparatus but in one case a building.

One such incident happened in the early 1980's and involved the Hills Ladder Truck. Upon returning from a call around Five A.M. on a cold Saturday December morning, Fire driver Jim Hoagerty pulled the apparatus in front of the Hills Firehouse applied the emergency brake and went inside to open the overhead door.

The James Hill Hook and Ladder Co. was named after James Hill, who in the 1800's was a city Alderman. He wasn't a member of the company, although his brother Bart was. This firehouse happened to be located on the crest of a hill at the foot of Third Street and Partition Street.

So when Jim parked the apparatus on top of the hill, he applied the mechanical brakes and had to walk inside the firehouse to open the overhead door manually. The city did not install remote overhead door openers until much later.

When Jim walked back outside, to his horror, the truck was gone. It was now rolling down the sidewalk toward the hollow. He truck glanced off a front porch on the right then headed to the left and glanced off a power pole. It did this twice until the intersection of Fifth Street and Partition Street. The truck was now heading directly for the home of Mrs. Mae Hockles.

By all rights the truck should have crashed right through the house and continued down into the hollow. The most amazing thing happened. The house had a set of concrete steps that went down into the front of the house from the sidewalk. The left front tire of the truck dropped onto the steps and stopped dead in its tracks and became wedged. The front porch roof was jammed completely through the trucks windshield, which probably helped to slow the truck down.

I had heard the call on my scanner and was at the scene in about fifteen minutes.

What a sight it was seeing that huge truck halfway down that hill with the entire front porch roof sticking out through what was once the cab and windshield like something out of a movie.

The most amazing thing was what didn't happen. When the truck slammed into the house, Mrs. Hockles was asleep on her couch in the front room. Besides getting the living hell scared out of her she never got as much as a scratch.

After the initial shock wore off, a tow truck was called and the recovery was about to begin. In true city fashion, the first tow truck call was made to "Willis Church". Old timers will remember old Willis Church, he had been around long enough to tow Gods first car! His tow truck was nothing more than a glorified pickup truck.

He was sent on his way and Robert's Towing was called. Soon they were on the scene. Once everything was stabilized, the tow truck was hooked up and Roberts slowly started winching the truck up the hill.

Everyone knows of "Murphy's Law" and in true fashion, Murphy's Law kicked in. About halfway up the hill the cable snapped on the tow truck. There goes the ladder truck back down the hill. This time we all thought for sure that the truck would make it down into the hollow taking Mrs. Hockles home with it.

But low and behold, the truck went back down the hill and into the same exact spot. Right into the same concrete stairs and came to rest again.

You can't make this stuff up. This really happened. There's no video like there would be today, but there are pictures around to this day. I have some myself as well as some newspaper clippings.

After the truck finally made its way to the top of the hill, we stripped it of all the gear and equipment and anything else that wasn't tied down. We really thought at the time that we had seen the last of that truck.

The truck was first towed to JGL Truck Repair in Watervliet and then to Robert's Body Shop also in Watervliet. It was eventually decided that the truck would be sent to Tyler Fire Repair in Brunswick, where it would slowly be repaired. The cab would be replaced with a used 1963 American LaFrance 900 Series cab and a complete air brake system would be installed. Of course had the truck been equipped with air brakes like it should have been in the first place, the accident probably wouldn't have happened. To not have air brakes in a vehicle that large was just plain crazy. But we were talking about the City of Rensselaer.

It took about eight months before the truck was repaired and placed back in service.

In the meantime, the city decided it would try and acquire a rental truck. One was eventually found available in Watertown N.Y. There was a whole group of us waiting for the truck the night it arrived so we could stow all the gear and equipment. When I first saw the truck coming down Third Street I said to myself it'll never fit in the firehouse, it was huge. It was a circa 1970's 100 Foot Seagraves Aerial and it almost didn't fit in the building. The only way it did was to have the ladder controls held in the down position with rubber straps.

A few tense moments concerning the Seagrave Rental Truck.

One Saturday morning I was at the Hills downstairs at the bar, Chris Yonkos was the on duty driver of the day. A call came in on the fire phone. I picked up the bar extension to listen to what the call was. Turns out it was off duty Fire Driver Mark Scradera, neighbor of my parents. And he was reporting a chimney fire at my parents' house. After hanging up the fire phone, I frantically ran out the side door to my pickup, grabbed my gear and jump in the cab of the truck. Chris goes to start the truck and click, click, click. The fucking truck won't start and I am saying holy shit my parents' house is on fire and this fucking truck won't start. After about a half of a minute Chris remembers that there are two starter switches and both had to be pushed at the same time. The truck starts and off we go. Thankfully the fire had not amounted to much and was quickly put out. This was one of those scary moments thinking your parents' home is on fire and the ladder truck is down.

In the early 1990's, while I was still working as a relief driver, I had a mishap of my own.

Late one morning, I was on duty at Pumper 3 on East Street. We received a call for a man with difficulty breathing at the Amtrak station. Pumper 2 was closed that day because of budget cuts so Pumpers 3 and 4 were dispatched. Fellow fire driver Richie McDougal, who was hanging out at the firehouse that morning and I jumped in the truck and began to respond. Now whenever you had to respond to a call in the City's North End from Pumper 3 (the Harts Firehouse) you had to pull out of quarters and make a 180° turn to go north on East Street. This was not an easy task because the 1961 pumper did not have power steering, so you had creep along slowly as you struggled with the steering wheel.

As we entered the intersection of East Street and Herrick Street a car appeared out of nowhere flying southbound down East Street. It ran the red light and slammed into the left front of pumper. Now the truck was moving slowly forward but the car hit us so hard that I pushed the truck backward about two feet. When all was said and done there were only minor injuries. The driver of the car was issued seven tickets that included speeding, running a red light, no seat belt, expired license and registration and no insurance. He also had a minor passenger in the car.

As far as the pumper, it would be out of service for several months while it was repaired. During this time it was replaced by a reserve pumper that was on loan to the city by the City of Albany. This truck had been on loan to replace Pumper 2 which had been out of service because of serious problems with its frame. This pumper had responded to hundreds of off road calls over the years for brush fires, bonfires etc. Pumper 2 had been repaired and recently been placed back in service.

The city used this loaner truck for all it was worth until one day while responding to a call in the city's lower end, the transmission blew on it leaving a trail of parts strewn down Broadway with fire driver Eddie Runion at the wheel. The city then sent the truck back to Albany as is.

Some of the craziest times concerning fire apparatus back in the mid to late 1970's occurred with the 1947 American LaFrance Ladder truck. This truck was used as the City's back up for the 1968 Ladder Truck until circa 1977. At the time, this truck was stored at the City's Public Works garage at Willow and Lawrence Streets. It was seldom used and not very well cared for. In fact, during this time, there were some very valuable things stolen from off the truck.

Such as the American LaFrance Fomite Emblem from the nose of the truck and a rare old generator that ran on white gas. It's amazing that the bell on the truck survived. Especially because today chrome plated brass bell can sell for $800.00 to $1000.00.

Anyway, whenever the truck was needed, it was a real crap shoot as to how she was going to run and operate.

On one such night, there was a large group of us at the firehouse when a call came in for a structure fire at Broadway and Pine Street. Denny Ellery was the driver that night and this would be one of his first but not last tough times with this truck. They just plain and simple didn't get along. So we all jump on the truck and all set to go and click, click, click. The truck would not start dead batteries.

So what to do? We decide to try and pop the clutch, and it's a good thing there were a lot of us because this truck was heavy and when you pulled out of the firehouse there was a slight uphill grade. Anyway it worked and off we went.

After the fire was extinguished, we soon had another problem with the truck. It had stalled out on Broadway because of all the lights draining what was left in the already near dead batteries. So here we go again, we try popping the clutch again, all of us right down Broadway. But this time she doesn't want to start. We push and push and push, all the way from Broadway and Pine Street to Broadway and Central Avenue, about a mile. Still no go. Along comes off duty fire driver Gorge Forget in his personal vehicle and a set of jumper cables. The truck finally starts and makes it back to quarters.

On election nights, the city was full of activity. Back then, Bon Fires throughout the city were the norm and such that the 1968 Ladder Truck did not respond to calls unless it was absolutely needed. It was used for radio communications to dispatch the pumpers.

On these nights the 1947 Ladder Truck was brought up and placed in service in case of a structure fire. The second man at the Hills was assigned to the 1947 truck if needed. Well on one such election night it was needed.

During the course of the evening we received a call for a structure fire for what was, at that time, Barnett Mills. This is where the Hilton Center is now. Denny Ellery was the second man on that night and off we went. Upon arrival, sure enough, one of the buildings had been torched and the fire was going good.

Denny had the truck positioned and had raised the Aerial Ladder with Dan Boomhower climbing the ladder. All of a sudden POW, a hydraulic line blows on the turntable and covers Denny from head to toe with hydraulic fluid. And as the ladder slowly dropped down all I can remember is Denny taking off his glasses and all you could see were his two eye balls peeking out from behind all of that oil. Denny and that truck just did not get along.

In 1977 the city decided to discard their reserve fire apparatus, and after much discussion the Hills Fire Company purchased the truck from the city for one dollar.

We were lucky at the time to have a place to store it thanks to one of our members, Dave Raid, who at the time was working at the Scotia Navel Depot as a federal fireman. For about twenty years we were able to keep the truck in an abandoned fire house on the depot grounds. The building was even heated. Once we took ownership of the truck one of our members, Dick Keneally took charge of repairs and up keep of the vehicle. We had new tires installed, had the cab repainted, the seats recovered etc.

Over the years we took the truck all over the northeast. Some of the best times were going to Firemen's Conventions. We would spend the weekend in different places such as Lake George and Lake Placid. As a company, we usually rented an entire motel and grounds and this was a "Family" event. Twice we even had the truck transported to Lake Placid via flatbed.

This truck was a very familiar site at parades all over. There were only about one hundred of these trucks manufactured, with Rensselaer receiving the last one made. There are very few left and ours may have been the last one still on the road. The only other one that can still be seen in this area is in the New York State Museum in the fire service exhibit. That truck came from the Watervliet Arsenal Fire Department where it served for many years.

In 1982 American La France was celebrating its 150th Anniversary with a Two Year calendar with pictures of twelve of their fire apparatus past and present. Since our truck was rare and in such good condition, it was selected to be one of the twelve.

After twenty some years, we were notified by the Scotia Navel Depot that we could no longer store our truck there. With no other place readily available to store a fifty foot long truck and a declining interest in parades, the company offered the truck to the Fireman's Museum in Hudson N.Y. They readily accepted and it's been there ever since and probably will be forever.

I had probably logged more miles on that truck than anyone else driving it back and forth to dozens and dozens of parades and I can tell you that this was one of the toughest trucks I've ever driven. With the large front tires behind the driver and the weight of the large engine directly over the front axle and, of course, no power steering getting around with this truck seemed to be something of an event. When this truck was in service it must have been quite a feat getting that truck around some of the narrow streets and tight turns of this city. The other tough thing about driving that truck was where the shift lever was located. It was right between the driver and the engine. It came up through the engine cover which was removable.

The driver's side of the engine cover was slanted and it was slotted in the shape of the shift pattern. And because it was slotted, the hot air from the engine and radiator was blown directly on the driver. This was fine in cold weather but it was like torture driving in those summertime parades.

One wild time we had with this truck was on one of the trips we made to Bennington, Vermont for their Vermont State Firemen's Convention. This was a great time and a large group of members rode the truck over, hanging all over it as usual. After marching in the parade we stuck around a while for our beer and hot dogs, and then we started making our way back to Rensselaer. Away we went barreling over Route 7 with a half of beer tapped right on the turntable of the truck. Just try and get away with a stunt like that today.

I was driving the truck that day and as we were coming down Interstate 787 going thru Menands, the guys started screaming for a bathroom break. So I pulled the truck over on the shoulder of 787 at Four O'clock on a Saturday afternoon and twenty guys lined up along the guard rail and let it rip.

Once back in the city, the norm was for the guys to start yelling hit the button, meaning sound the Federal Siren. So here were going down Washington Avenue then over Third Street past a packed St. Joseph's Church with the doors wide open riding by with the Federal Siren screaming. Chances were the mayor was probably in attendance. Anyway it was back to the firehouse for party time.

Guys today would probably think that this was outrageous behavior, and today it would be, but back then it wasn't even an afterthought. It's just the way things were done at that time.

As far as parades go, we always had a great time where ever we were, whether it is Lake George, Lake Placid or Saugerties, in the late seventies, where it rained so hard that we wound up marching in a foot and a half of water. We had gone to dozens of local Parades and Parade Weekends where the members, wives and girlfriends always had the best of times. And as usual the beer and liquor flowed and there was always enough food to feed a small army.

We always tried to do the best we could while marching in the parades. It would have been so great to have won a trophy in one of the big convention parades. We never did but I really believe that we came close on more than one occasion. We did however manage to win two or three trophies in the City's Memorial Day Parade during the years we marched and, even one, when I was the Parade Captain.

And, as always, after our local parades we always made our way back to the fire house bar room for proper refreshments for the members and their families. We also always had a standing invitation to the Visiting fire companies from our outlying districts such as East Greenbush, Defreestville, Clinton Heights and even Green Island. They always enjoyed the hospitality along with the hot dogs and beer.

These events were always terrific times because it involved not only the member's wives, girlfriend, extended families and guests, but also involved the children of all ages who always had the time of their lives. A lot of the children would wind up becoming members of the firehouse themselves when they came of age which I believe is a testament to the way we did things back then. On a side note, every year the company put on a really great Christmas Party for the members and their wives and girlfriends.

In my opinion it was always the best party of the year. I guess I am a little bias because I ran most of them. For many years on the afternoon of the adult's party, we also put on a Christmas Party for the members children. This party was always a wonderful success and we provided the soda, snacks, pizza and gifts for every child. One of the more full-figured members would dress up as Santa and the on-duty driver would call out of service and take Santa up the street and out of sight. The kids were brought up to the apparatus floor and wait for Santa to arrive. It was always quite a sight to see all the children lined up at the overhead door peering out in great anticipation.

Once the kids saw St. Nick coming down Third Street standing on the running board of the truck, they just went wild. When things finally settled down, Santa would come downstairs and meet with all the kids one by one, putting each one on his lap and handing out a present to one and all. Of course while all this was going on the adults were enjoying the warm hospitality of the bar area.

Now back to the parades. I think some of the greatest times at the many parades always were the St. Patrick's Day Parades. These were always my personal favorites. We began attending the St. Patrick's Day Parades first by going to the Troy Parade. The turnout was great and we always had a tremendous time. After each one of these yearly parades would always wind up at the South Troy Hibernian Hall and they always treated us like gold. We were always welcome there with plenty of beer and hot beef stew. That worked out perfect since the day of the parade was usually cold, wet and or snowy.

Sometimes after we left the Troy Hibernian Hall we would venture across the Hudson over to Watervliet and visit their Hibernian Hall, where again we were always more than welcome.

Keep in mind, all of this traveling around was done with one vehicle, the 1947 Ladder Truck. This again was another one of those times that we were hopping all over the Capitol District with fifteen or twenty intoxicated firemen hanging all over the truck. Remember, back then, the police wouldn't bother a bunch of firemen as long as no one started trouble or nobody got hurt.

Anyway, after many years of having a fantastic time, the powers that be thought that we should start attending the Albany Parade. One of these guys had said that he knew some people and could pull some string to get us into their parade. So the company bought into it and we started going to the Albany Parade. The first year we went, we wound up being the last participant in the parade. That was okay because after all we were the new kids on the block and that was fine and we still had a good time.

The bad part was, there was no Hibernian Hall at the end of the parade and also no hot beef stew. But, as usual, there was always going back to the fire house and plenty of beer and corned beef and cabbage. So year after year we continued to go back to the Albany Parade and it was always a good time. For some reason we always wound up bringing up the rear of the parade, and that was fine with us because we always had plenty to drink as always and it was all about fun, and we knew how to have it. The funny part was that, we found out years later why we always bringing up the rear of the parade.

Turns out the member who had told us about knowing somebody and pulling some strings was full of shit and we were never officially part of the parade, we had just been pretty much tagging along. So much for the new powers that be!

STARTING DOWNHILL

One summer in the early 1990's, Mayor Horrigan and the Drivers' Union Local were having some difficult times. They were locking horns about health and safety issues such as fire escapes on certain firehouses. Diesel fumes from the apparatus and also from the Amtrak Trains and the damage being done to the drivers ears from Federal Q Sirens among other things. The mayor was seeing red over these issues and was looking for any reason for revenge.

One summer day I was working the A-shift in the Hills Firehouse when right after radio check I received a call on the house phone from Chuck Braver, who was working in the Hart Hose. Chuck tells me that City D.P.W. workers had just arrived at the Harts Fire House and had orders, from the mayor, to move the drivers bedroom from upstairs to down stairs into the old bar room at the rear at the apparatus floor. He also tells me that when they were done there, the Hills were their next stop.

So Chuck says to me I don't know about you Bill but I am going home sick. I tell Chuck, that being a relief driver, I didn't really have that option that I'll just have to stay and see how it all plays out. Now at the Harts Firehouse moving the bedroom downstairs wasn't all that bad because aside from needing a good cleaning the old bar was a good sized room with a bathroom and two doors for egress. It just needed a shower which was added later on.

But the Hills Firehouse was a whole other story. There was no extra room downstairs or anywhere else in the fire house. There was only about fifteen feet of extra space behind the rear of the ladder truck and the driver's kitchen. Well that's exactly where the city workers were ordered to move the bedroom to. Right out in the open, right behind the fuckin ladder truck. This was all very hard to believe but that's what the mayor wanted and he was dead serious. So after an hour or so the driver bedroom now shared the apparatus floor with the apparatus.

It didn't take very long for news of this to echo through the city and I started getting phone calls and visitors dropping by to see it for themselves. One of the visitors was Officer Steve Pohl of the Rensselaer Police Department, and an old friend of mine. He was also a member of the Hill Hooks. Right away he starts busting my balls asking if it was okay if he came into my bedroom. I've seen a lot of crazy things go on in this city and fire department but this one was right near the top of the list.

Anyway the bedroom stayed behind the truck all afternoon until around Five O'clock when I received a call on the house phone. And it was Mayor Horrigan himself. To tell that it was OK to move the bedroom back upstairs. Except this time there were no city employees to do the move, only me. I was however able to enlist the help from some of the Hills members. P.S. The bedroom at the Harts Firehouse remained on the apparatus floor behind the truck until the city closed the building many years later.

Well if that incident was right near the top of the list, this one will take the blue ribbon.

Later that same summer I was working in the Hills Firehouse, not sure what shift it was. A little while past radio check, a flatbed truck from Curtis Lumber pulled up to the firehouse and backed in to the parking lot. It was loaded with all kinds of pressure treated lumber. 2x4s, 4x4s stair stringers etc.

I go out and ask the driver what all this was for. And he says it was ordered by Wainschaif Associates, a local contractor. And it was for a fire escape, a wooden fire escape, on a firehouse of all places. A wooden fucking fire escape.

So I tell the guy that I do not know anything about it and he drops the load and away he goes. I try calling the chief first but, as usual, no answer. Next, I called the City Clerk's Office and spoke to Maureen Darnacci, the City Clerk and also a member of the Public Safety Board. Maureen said that she knew nothing about this but would look into it and get back to me. After a little while Maureen called back to say that apparently this was a deal between the City's Building Inspector and Wainshaif associates.

Anyway the deal was nixed and eventually Curtis Lumber was back to pick up their wood and that was the end of the wooden fire escape saga.

At some point later on, an all steel fire escape was constructed on the east side of the firehouse that exited from the meeting room to the ground level.

But the City of Rensselaer N.Y. came very close to being the first city anywhere to have a wooden fire escape on a working fire house.

Chris Yonkos one of the fire driver at the Hills Firehouse and he was assigned to the D-shift. Chris was the type of guy that would love to keep busy between calls. When off duty Chris and fellow driver Gorge Forget were house painters, interior and exterior and they were very good at it. Being a painter Chris would always try to keep the fire house, truck and equipment looking good.

One summer Chris had been touching up the silver on the truck such as the running boards and other diamond plates parts. While on a roll, Chris thought it would be a good idea to paint the fire phone at the front of the apparatus floor silver. After all it looked old and was a dull black. Well I guess because the weather which had been hot and muggy, the silver paint hadn't completely dried on the ear piece.

The next morning after Chris had been relieved by Jim East of the A-shift; Easty answered the fire phone and wound up with a silver right ear for the better part of the day.

Another time while the city was celebrating its bicentennial, Chris was in another mischievous painting mood. He thought it might be a good idea to paint the traditionally silver running boards on the ladder truck gold. It did look pretty strange and Easty who was totally anal about the trucks appearance went ballistic. So after he had scratched his balls, his head, his chest, he finally calmed down and eventually got the running boards back to silver. The truck wasn't the only thing Chris gave a paint job to in the firehouse.

On a spring Saturday afternoon, back in the hey day, Chris enlisted the help of good friend and fellow firehouse member Dick Keneally to give his car a paint job. Chris pulled the truck out, shut the overhead door, taped up all the windows on the apparatus floor and they painted Chris's car bright yellow. After that the car was fondly called the Fire Department Taxi.

One of the most beloved drivers the fire department ever had was Don Bossey. Don was one of the nicest, easy going and a good natured man there ever was. He was a true gentleman's gentleman with a great sense of humor. I had the good fortune of knowing Don for a good part of my life, first by growing up in his neighborhood, being his paper boy for several years, to joining the fire department and working with him as both a Volunteer Fireman and working with him for a few years as a relief driver.

On one of Don's last days on the job I was working the A-shift in the Hart Hose Firehouse. I was asked by fire drivers John Hull and Mike Mund to join them to give Don the traditional fire department send off. John, Mike and I all pulled up facing the front of the Rings Firehouse with Pumpers 2, 3 and 4 with the Federal Sirens blaring for a good five minutes or so. To this day I have been honored to have been asked to be part of this small but sincere send off. Unfortunately, after only a few short years of retirement, we lost Don at far too early an age.

Another of the fire drivers who was a real character was Fred Van Amps. Fred was kind of a throw back in the fire department. He was an avid hunter and fisherman and the type of guy who would give you the shirt off his back and he loved his beer. Fred was someone that we had a lot of fun and a lot of laughs with over the years. He was another guy that we lost at an early age.

Steve Falls was a true Rensselaer original. He was much better known as T-Falls.

T-Falls was kind of a legend around the city even in his younger days. He was very mechanically inclined and he could build or repair almost anything. I'll never forget when I was a kid and seeing his picture in the newspaper. He had welded three bicycle frames together and ran three chains to each one. The bike was so tall that he had to get on it from his front porch roof. And that's exactly what he did, and he actually rode it around the streets.

Later on his life he became a very talented heavy equipment operator and over the road truck driver. He was into the whole "monster truck" thing before it became popular.

But he didn't go and watch it in some arena; he actually went out and did it in real swamps and mud boggs. He had two full size Ford Broncos and had modified them himself. They both had giant oversize tires on them and one of them he called his recovery vehicle. On the front of it there was a large brush guard and wrapped around it was a long length of inch rope that had been liberated from some tug boat.

He was also an active member of Pumper Four who fought the many fires that we had back then. Much like Fred Van Amps he was a hard drinker and loved his fun and adventure. He could also be one funny son of a bitch. A comedian that could imitate almost anyone, mostly other members of the fire department.

Whenever he stopped by the bar at the Hills, he wouldn't hesitate to start imitating Big Joe Forceful, right in front of him. T-Falls was one of a very few that could get away with this with Big Joe. He would have the entire bar in stitches.

Another guy that "T" would love to imitate was retired police Sargent Nino Capriati who had had throat surgery that had left a hole in his throat and he had to speak through a hand held speaker. So "T" would start imitating Nino by grabbing a TV remote, hold it up to his throat and start making noises that were spot on to what Nino sounded like. I know it sounds like a very cold thing to do but goddamn it was fuckin funny.

T-Falls was another guy who would give you the shirt off his back and help out anyone who needed it. He was another true Rensselaer Original and another guy that not only died much too soon but also of strange circumstances.

"T" had been suffering from a bad tooth for a while and apparently had no plans to see a dentist. I am sure he was probably self-medicating with booze and who knows what else. At some point he sat down in his living room chair and probably passed out. Apparently the tooth was an abscessed tooth that had become infected, sending poison throughout his blood stream. He died right there in that living room chair. It was about a week before his body was found. He was found by police officer Bob Waiter who had been checking on his well-being.

After repeated try's ringing the doorbell to no avail, Bob placed a nearby extension ladder to a second floor window. He then saw what he thought was the body of an African American man dead in the living room chair. It turned out to be the body of T-Falls, who had sat down and died of a tooth infection. What a strange way for such a wild and talented individual to go.

There were a lot of people who would have considered him as a troublemaker, bad influence, screw ball etc. But he was always up front and honest and you always knew where he was coming from.

Probably the most familiar character in the fire department is a guy who has been hanging out at the fire houses for over forty years and is still around today. Bub Grunt has been a member of the James Hill Hook and Ladder for over four decades. And he's been well known by just about every driver and volunteer from all the companies over all those years.

Bub is known for his general goofiness, endless sense of humor, the butt of many jokes and his crazy imitations that he's done of all the drivers and a lot of members over the years. Bub has been the whipping boy of almost everyone around him for many years. But Bub is a terrific sport who could not only take the abuse; he could give it right back.

I still love to tell him to this day that he and the 1947 ladder truck have one thing in common. They're both the same age and are both ugly as hell. He loves it. Bub is still hanging around today doing the same things he's always done, except his audience is getting smaller.

Around the early to mid-1990's, the city had the brilliant idea to turning Pumper One and Pumper Two into all volunteer companies, meaning volunteer drivers. This move would prove to be a disaster and anyone who chose to be a volunteer driver was instantly considered a scab or union busters. One way it didn't work was that the paid drivers didn't acknowledge them and made sure that they weren't needed by not giving them too many runs if any at all. A lot of the permanent drivers also considered the relief drivers as scabs, but to us it was a bad rap. We were only trying to be appointed to a full time position and being a relief driver was considered a stepping stone. In fact most of the permanent drivers had started out as relief drivers before their permanent appointment. I guess they just all had very short memories. Over time this plan was abandoned to the relief of almost everyone. To this day there are at least four paid drivers on the job today that started out as relief drivers.

In 1992, when it became apparent that I would never get a permanent appointment to the fire department, I decided it was time to resign my position and move on to a new job with the New York State Department of Transportation. After almost twenty years of being one of the most active firemen in the city, I decided it was time to give up an active fireman's role and become more of a social member in the firehouse. This was just the way it was back then in the city, guys got older, slowed down and moved on and the younger guys took over. The only problem was that the trend was starting where there were fewer and fewer young people that were interested in getting involved with becoming a volunteer fireman.

The state had begun imposing more and more mandatory training making it less appealing to young people. This was becoming a nationwide issue, not just a local problem.

Back in our day, it was having a bar that was our compensation. And that was something of an attraction to lure the younger guys to join the fire department. But more and more towns, villages and municipalities were doing away with having bars in firehouses.

One way some fire departments have tried to compensate the volunteers was to offer some sort of a pension if they stayed active long enough and were active enough.

Nowadays, even in the City of Rensselaer, they have begun Junior Firefighter Programs to try to bring young people, both boys and girls into the fire department. The program seems to be working and this will probably be the future of the fire department.

Now back when I had said that I was one of the most active firemen in the city, I am talking almost exclusively about the blaze days of the mid to late 1970's and into the 1980's. I fought these fires first as a fireman and then most of them as a fire officer. Unfortunately, other than the drivers log books, there were virtually no records that were kept as far as what volunteers did and what fires they fought.

I was actually active enough that when Assistant Fire Chief Joe Buono was planning to retire he lobbied the Board of Public Safety to give me his job. Unfortunately because of politics that never happened.

Besides being very active in the fire department in general, I was also very active within my own company, the James Hill Hook and Ladder. From the time I joined in 1974 right on through the 2000's, at one time or another I had held just about every office within the company.

I was honored to have been chosen to be Company President during our 100th Anniversary in 1992, also serving, chaired and co-chaired many committees. In the fall of 1995, after what many of us considered the dark year, or the year that never happened, I was appointed by then Company President and good friend, Jim Hockles, as bar and house chairman at the James Hill Hook and Ladder. I would spend the next twelve plus years busting my ass providing beer, liquor, snacks etc. to the members of the Hills Fire House.

It was I job that I loved and I prided myself on trying to keep everyone happy. In all that time, I worked very hard to try and keep prices down while costs were constantly on the rise. This was of course a very thankless job and in January of 2007, after a total disagreement with the new President Mike Forget, I decided to turn in my keys and walk away for good. After another fruitless meeting with him one night I walked out and never went back. I guess he thought his new ideas of total accountability were a better way to go, but what he wanted was way over the top.

The more time goes by and I look back on it I think that the accountability thing was just a way to push me out. Over the years I had always had the support of many of my friends. This time they were nowhere to be found. One of my favorite old sayings is "If it ain't broke don't fix it." And it turned out to be so true because within a few months the bar was in complete disarray, so much for accountability. I guess I had been doing something right.

It didn't matter much anyway because in August of 2007 the city decided to end the practice of serving alcohol in any city buildings mainly firehouses. While it was very unpopular with the members, it was something that was inevitable. It had lasted much longer than anybody thought it would and due to insurance liability problems the city had to put an end to it. By choice my days in the fire department had come down to nothing more than in name in January 2007. Because of an inept president and the fact that most of my supporters had turned their backs on me, I figured that these proposed changes were being put forth. I was starting to get the feeling of being burned out after all the years I had been giving all my time to the firehouse bar. Between all the time I was putting in, the wear and tear on my personal vehicle and all the gas I was using, it made the decision to walk away that much easier. When I look back on it all now, I not only wonder how I did but I wonder why I did it.

As I mentioned this was a very thankless job and there were always a lot more complaints than compliments. The only person that has a good idea of what doing the bar chairman's job is Chris Yonkos having done it himself for twenty five years. I think it's funny that shortly after I gave up the chairman's position; it didn't take long for some of my replacements to start crying for gas money, something that I never asked for in my twelve years.

On a side note, the bar itself at the fire house which was updated in the early 1970's, just before I became a member, was getting a little tattered by the late 1990's and into the 2000's. But it was still nice and comfortable. It was homey, with a lot of memorabilia. And there was always a bone of contention with it about one thing. You had to enter the bar at one end by ducking down on the west end of it and was always a pain in the ass to crouch down under that end of the bar; even more so for older members.

This debate went on and on for years, until once Mike Forget became president and the decision was made to cut the bar. Now I'll always admit that I was always one of the ones that were totally against cutting the bar, once it was done it was like a breath of fresh air. Especially to the older members and some of the middle aged members. It made things a hell of a lot easier, and the job was done very nicely. But being the very superstitious person that I am, and looking back on it now I honestly believe that cutting the bar without a doubt. Jinxed the fate of the firehouse. It was time to go.

The only thing that I regret about from all those years that I put into the fire department is that I put it first and my family second a lot of the time, and for that I am truly sorry, and that's something I can never get back.

Most people that came through the fire department stayed around a few years while some lasted a little longer.

My run had lasted the better part of three decades.

With the bar now closed the members still had complete use of the fire house, the rec room, meeting room. But that was pretty much it. The writing was on the wall, plain as day or so it should have been. I had been preaching to the company membership for many years that the day was going to come sooner or later that the firehouse bar days would come to an end one way or another.

There was more and more talk about the city building a new fire house in the North End. Talk like this took place on and off throughout the city for decades with it always ending up as false promises. But this time it appeared that it might really happen, this time the city actually had property on which to build. Sure enough in 2009 the city broke ground on a brand new three bay firehouse on Washington Avenue at the entrance to the monastery. It was all but a sure thing that the ladder truck would be moved to the north end station.

Now the next string of events is exactly why the membership of the Hills should have started removing property from the firehouse and kept it in safe keeping.

One morning in 2010 the end of the old firehouse on partition street was about to come to fruition. The on duty driver at the Hills had gone from the main building where the semi reserve pumper was being housed next door to the make shift fire house where the ladder truck lived, for now. He had gone over to wash the ladder truck, once he had finished he went back over to the main firehouse only to find a heavy smoke condition on the apparatus floor. At some point a fire had started in the driver's kitchen and was going good. After reporting the fire, getting the pumper off the apparatus floor to hook it up to the hydrant across the street at Third and Partition Street and the arrival of other apparatus, the damage was pretty extensive.

When it was all said and done the building, almost 120 years old was a total loss.

The firehouse membership still had a lot of property left in the building stored throughout the firehouse, but now had no access to the building. In my mind the company should have seen the handwriting on the wall long before this incident and started removing company property and getting it to a safe place. Because of the fire this would be all but impossible now. I realize that quite a few members believed deep down that even when the city would move the ladder truck to the new firehouse that the city would sell the building to the membership for little or nothing.

But those days were over. The days of 1977 when the company was able to purchase the 1947 ladder truck for a dollar were long gone.

Only a few years before the city had closed the Hart Hose Firehouse and wound up selling that building for almost $125,000.00.

So now the building was deemed unsafe and none of the members were allowed inside. And all of the company's possessions were stuck inside.

Eventually the city would set up a time and date for the membership to be allowed in to retrieve their belongings. But even when they did, everything wasn't taken. It is my understanding that the beer coolers and the pool table were left behind. And I am left wondering why. Was this because of laziness, or the lack of preplanning or because nobody really gave a shit.

When it was all said and done, the city wound up getting only $15,000.00 for the firehouse, much less than anyone had expected, but also a hell of a lot more than a buck.

Anyway the city did a real nice job on the building of the new firehouse.

But from what I hear is the only problem with it that it's not very volunteer or even people friendly. Apparently if you're not a part of the in crowd, you're not very welcome to hang out like you used to be able to in the old firehouses. Company meetings can be held there, but as soon as the meetings is over you have to leave. You're not wanted there.

After a while the Hills membership decided to start holding their meetings at the Gerald O'Neil American Legion Post on Broadway. At least there they could have a few beers, relax, have a few laughs and loosen up. From what I hear even retired drivers who were always a fixture at the old firehouses, stopping by for a cup of coffee, shoot the shit or just bust some balls. Apparently they are not even welcome.

When I first joined the fire department in 1974 at the age of seventeen I had the utmost respect for the paid drivers, I had always been taught to respect your elders. The fire department is a whole different one than the one that I knew and loved.

My time in the fire department has been over for several years now. I am still a member of the James Hill Hook and Ladder Co, but in name only.

I don't really care for the fire department that I see today, but that's mostly because I am a very old school type of person that does not adapt well to change. So all I can do at this point is to keep in contact with some of my closest old buddies about the good old days, which we do often. Just because what I see in the fire department today doesn't mean it's bad I don't mean that at all, it's just my opinion.

And I would never wish ill will on the fire department of any time frame; I have too much respect for what firefighters do day in and day out.

I just really wish that the fire house members and paid drivers of today would show some of that respect to the members and drivers of the past and what they did and what they went through, we all deserve at least that.

How about mutual respect, that should work.

ON THE CITY'S DIME

I've often wondered that year after year and decade after decade of the firehouse bars in the City of Rensselaer, if any of the city officials ever had a clue of what the bars were costing them.

In the Hill Hooks, the bar alone had two beer coolers, a soda machine, a soda machine turned beer machine and a refrigerator, all running twenty four hours a day, seven days a week, 365 days a year. Not to mention, all the lights that were left on most of the time, three televisions and three air conditioners running around the clock in the summer months.

Up until 1988, when the city closed the Pumper Four firehouse, this was going on in five firehouses, for decades.

While most of the city officials always knew what was going on in the fire house bars, the fact is that they just kept on paying those Niagara Mohawk/National Grid Bills without ever questioning it once, to my knowledge. These bills must have been enormous most of the time.

All this just tells me what most people had suspected for years. A complete and total lack of accountability.

If it does turn out the city officials were aware of what they were paying for, let me be the first of many hundreds and hundreds of firehouse members to give city hall a Huge Thank You and maybe even a little hug!

A DVD AND MISSING THINGS

Recently, the Hills Fire Company put together a bunch of newer and old photos of parades, parties, dinners, firehouse weekends etc., some of these pictures dated back to the 1800's. The company had these photos made into a picture DVD, kind of a history of the firehouse and its members.

A lot of good memories and it turned out to be really terrific. I found it interesting though that in all of those pictures there was only one photo of an actual fire. I would like to say that there is a good reason for that but there's not. In fact there is a very bad reason for it.

At one time the company had a really great collection of fire scenes that had occurred over the years. In the late seventies and early eighties, more and more members of the companies were becoming fire buffs and a lot of them started their own personal museums. Certain items started to disappear from the fire houses. This of course included just about any picture that had anything to do a fire scene.

It's bad enough that these pictures were stolen, but in later years, when a few books were released in the city that included fire photos, some of these pictures actually showed up in these books. And certain people had the incredible gall to take credit for the pictures. So for anyone wondering where all of the pictures of all of those fire scenes that I spoke earlier about are, there's your answer.

The other really bad thing about these pictures and other items that had come up missing is that the membership is about 99.5% sure that at least one of our own members is responsible for taking these items. Unfortunately the Hills Fire Company could never prove these suspicions even though the police department had been consulted several times. At one point in the early 1990's, I even had a badge stolen off my fire department jacket that was being stored in the basement of my own house. Again, although I am still 100% certain of who is responsible for this incident, it could never be proven. Sadly these events were somewhat common place around this time frame.

In the early 1990's, Relief Driver John Lefflaw was working in the Harts Firehouse on East Street. While upstairs in the bedroom, he heard someone enter the apparatus floor and thought it was just someone stopping by for a visit. Then, before he knew it, he heard the door on the apparatus open and shut and the person exit the firehouse. By the time John made his way down to the apparatus floor to have a look around, he noticed his helmet was missing from the cab of the truck. It was not just an ordinary helmet. This helmet had belonged to his father who was a retired fire driver and it was also an antique. I'll bet if you ask John today he will tell you he's almost positive he knows who had taken it.

The sad truth of this is this. The individuals responsible for taking these items are nothing more than common thieves, criminals that by all rights that should have been prosecuted. These are the very things that give organizations a black eye and it's shameful.

Another incident took place back in the early 1990's when the city took the 1967 Minks Pumper out of service for the final time. After the truck had been stripped of all the equipment and anything else of use, the truck was parked outside the Broadway firehouse. Unfortunately, all of the bling on the truck, such as the American LaFrance signs, axe holders and assorted chrome pieces and fixtures had been left on the truck. This was like transmitting a three alarm hard on to the city fire buffs.

Can you just imagine if there was a Batroom back then, good God they would be taking guys out on stretchers? Holy shits what a freakin mess to clean up, somebody please order a trailer load of rubber gloves.

But anyway getting back to the truck, by the following morning it was picked as clean as a thanksgiving turkey. Word was quickly put out that if these items were returned A.S.A.P. there would be no questions asked. Eventually all was returned to the proper authorities. But in the long run where any or all of these items wound up, well that's anybody's guess. My guess is that there residing in one or more of the local museums. I wish these private museums would open their doors to the public once in a while, before of course, certain items are removed and hidden. There's at least one item I'd like to get back, no questions asked.

1992 THE HILLS 100TH ANNIVERSARY CELEBRATION

As I mentioned earlier, 1992 was the year the James Hill Hook and Ladder was about to celebrate its' One Hundredth Anniversary. The company had been gearing up for this celebration for many years planning many very special events to be held throughout the year.

Along with Chris Yonkos, the General Chairman of all events, and myself as Company President, Chris and I worked very close together and guided all of these events with great success. Every one of the events had a Chairman and a Committee appointed.

In all, the company had planned ten events starting with the regular Installation of Officers dinner held at the Polish American Citizens Center in Albany.

This was followed by the 100th Anniversary Dinner Dance held at the Desmond Americana, Colonie, New York. This was a very high class, black tie gala with an enormous turnout by every available company member, past and present. This event has many pictures depicted in the company's DVD that has been put together. Most members and wives and girlfriends made a weekend of the event by taking rooms at the Desmond for the weekend. The company pulled out all of the stops on this party and it was an incredible time.

Next up was the City's Annual Memorial Day Parade and Open House. This one turned out to be a total disaster because the weather just didn't cooperate, it was just horrible. It was cold, rain and just plain miserable. We all really thought it was going to snow, it was that bad. The company had planned to have a terrific showing at the parade, which it did, and then put on food and beverages at the end of the parade at Riverside Park. Afterward the fire house was going to put on an open house for the general public. Unfortunately, Mother Nature won out and the day was pretty much ruined.

Then it was off to the Catskills and The Friar Tuck Inn in June. This was another tremendous time with, again a terrific member turnout. This was the company's second trip down to the Friar Tuck, the first one being in 1977 for its 85th Anniversary and it was a classy joint, both times.

The next two events were much more casual get togethers, which in some ways were, more to the company's make up. On August 1st, the Hills had an Old Time Family Picnic at Camp Adventure, the Rensselaer Boys Club Camp at Burden Lake. Next was a cruise on the Hudson River in October aboard the now defunct St. Joseph's riverboat. Both of these events were more or less low keyed but of course a good time was had by all, as usual.

The last actual event to take place for the year was the Gala Christmas Party chaired by yours truly. This to me was always the best event of the year, and this one was no different, it was a very fitting end to a wonderful year at the Hills Firehouse.

Now I know I said there were ten events held that year, but I had just referred to seven of them. The other three were as follows.

Every first Saturday of month, which was always considered Couples Nite, would be a little more enhanced for the 100th Anniversary, which it was. Every one of those nites was a great time had by all and a great show of members, wives and girlfriends.

The ninth event that happened was the availability of the 100th Anniversary Programmed Book. This book was put together by longtime member and Officer Thom Pohl, who did a terrific job on this book.

Last, but not least, were the 100th Anniversary Fire House Coats. These coats wound up being a combination of heavy wool with leather sleeves and were great for the very cold winters of the northeast but were nothing more than a decoration for the other nine months of the year. Don't get me wrong these coats were very nice and very well made, but they were clearly a one season coat. They did, however, come in very handy at the Memorial Day Parade. Besides keeping the members warm, they made quite a statement while marching. This is pictured in the Company's new DVD.

A couple of other things that came out of the 100th Anniversary were as follows:

A new company logo was chosen for the event, and it was designed by the Company Foreman at the time Dave Santini. Dave did a very nice job on it, and it's still something to be very proud of today.

The year 1992 was also the year the company create an all new committee called The Capitol Improvement Committee. This committee was meant to come up with new ideas and improvements to the firehouse such as meeting rooms and the bar room. The original committee members were Chairman, Greg Yonkos Committee Members Glen Van Arnstine Jr, Bob Blay and Rick Ryemun.

The 100th Anniversary year of 1992 was all in all a huge success and every event and activity were thoroughly enjoyed by the entire membership, wives, girlfriends and guests alike.

The company had commemorative plates and glasses designed as part of the celebration. One of the better things to come out during the year was the 100th Anniversary Book. This task was taken on by Chairman Tom Pohl with seven other Company Officers and Members, along with me. Tom worked very hard, put long hours, months and the better part of a year on this book. The end result is a hard cover, complete history of the Fire Company and its Members. It acknowledges all of the Paid Drivers who had worked at the Hills Firehouse, the city's Fire Chiefs, entire Company Membership from 1892 to present, all the events and committees through the year and many great pictures from over the years and decades. Tom deserves a tremendous amount of credit for all the time and effort for this book and I was very happy to have been a small part of it.

BAZAARS AND FUND RAISERS

For many, many decades the main fund raiser of the year was the Annual Bazaar usually held in late May or the first part of June. We weren't the only company in the city to have bazaars.

The E.F. Hart Hose and Chemical Hose Co. Pumper Four also were holding the yearly event, along with one of the school's in the city. The three fire companies and the school would have to coordinate with each other so there would not be a conflict in the scheduling.

These events were a lot of work for the members who participated but it was even a lot more work for the bazaar chairman and other committee members. The chairman was almost always the current president.

When I first joined the company these bazaars were still going very strong and brought a lot of money in for the individual companies.

For many years, we would always kick off the bazaar on Thursday night with the Yankee Doodle Band coming up and performing a free concert in full uniform to the delight of everyone. Outside of the firehouse and on the apparatus floor there were plenty of carnival type games and also games geared toward children with toys and stuffed animals as prizes. These games were rented from year to year from usually shady outfits that seemed like they were about one step ahead of the law. But back then it all worked and everybody made their money. The membership operated the games and we were all glad that we only had to do this once a year.

These types of games were the big attraction but were not the real money maker. The real money was being made downstairs in the bar area where three or four poker tables were operating to all hours of the night. This was where the members who were dealing, shuffling the cards or counting money did the most work. If you did not shut down the games and make them leave, many games would last until five or six o'clock in the morning and the players would keep on playing. A lot of times when they left the firehouse the whole group would wind up at one of the players homes or apartment and just keep on playing. These people were all hard core poker players who all knew each other and pretty much had traveled the local circuit together. And once they had their seat at the table they did not want to leave it, for any reason.

We even had one player, who was a regular, who had to go to the bathroom really bad but would not leave the table. Finally he couldn't hold it anymore and pissed himself right there at the table and all over the floor.

But, like so many things and after years of running the bazaars without any oversight, the State of New York finally figured out that they were missing out on a lot of revenue. And as usual, once they got involved, it was all downhill from there.

The last bazaar we held at the Hill Hook and Ladder was in 1991, the year that I became company president. We weren't planning on having a bazaar that year because of the 100th Anniversary celebration. But it was during that year it was decided that the company would end the practice of having bazaars which really came as a relief to just about the entire membership.

The next big fundraising event that the company would venture into would be the Annual Super Bowl Raffle.

Beginning in February, the company would begin to distribute raffle tickets to the members and start to sell raffle tickets for the following years Super Bowl. The winner of the raffle would receive tickets to the big game, airfare to and from the games location, and provide lodging for five nights and six days. The initial cost for each ticket was $25.00 each and the raffle quickly became very popular for quite a few years. As with many raffles, there were guys who would sell just a few tickets per year to other members while there were others who would go beyond the call year after year.

One such member was one of my best friends for life Eddie Shore. Ed could be counted on to sell anywhere between fifty and one hundred tickets every year that we held this raffle.

For the first several years, the cost of the entire Super Bowl package was about $3,000.00, but as the years went on, the cost of the package began to steadily rise.

Two weeks before Super Bowl weekend we would put on a big party and anyone who had purchased a ticket would be able to come to the party for food, football and the grand drawing. We would put on snacks, pizza, 6ft. long subs and provide beer and soda.

This party was always held in conjunction with the NFC/AFC Championship Games. We always filled the room with televisions in every direction that you looked. We brought all of the T.Vs from the firehouse and we always rented at least two large screens T.V's to have on hand.

During the course of the afternoon, while the crowd was watching the football, eating and drinking, we had a small army of members walking around raffling off the unsold tickets. By doing this we always sold an additional fifty to seventy five tickets.

The grand drawing was always held during halftime of the second game of the afternoon.

This major fund raiser was very popular until the early to mid-2000's, when the price of the Super Bowl package began to exceed the Seven Thousand dollar mark. Between the inflating price of the Super Bowl package and the cost of trying to put on a party for the drawing, it became more and more difficult to just break even.

This was pretty much the end of any large fund raisers for the company and we were forced into a series of smaller raffles and relying more on slot machine revenue at the bar.

As long as they were kept in good working order the slot machines could provide the company with some good revenue. A lot of credit for keeping those machines going over the years goes to my brother Rick who was extremely handy with the repair and upkeep of them. When he was president of the company, Rick even arranged to have our original machine completely reconditioned and painted to almost brand new condition.

THE END

The era of having Five Separate Fire Companies has come to an end. The James Hill Hook and Ladders, E.F. Hart Hose and Pumper Four all reside at the new North End Station.

Only the G.S. Mink and T. Claxton Hose are still, at least for now, stationed in their own firehouse. The building that housed J.N.Ring has been sold and the truck decommissioned. The company still exists.

As I mentioned earlier in the book, the city did a nice job building the North End Station. The only thing I think that has been done poorly is the location. It's simply in the wrong part of the city. The bulk of fire protection is now housed in the north end of the city, while in the south end of the city below Partition Street is where almost all of the business and industry resides.

The city should have tried much harder to find a location in the middle of the city. The north end of the city had long needed a fire house, but one pumper would have been suitable.

Having firehouses spread out through the city was done for a reason. Each neighborhood had some form of fire protection and much quicker response time along with some piece of mind.

I realize that this way of thinking is old school and not very cost effective. The trend today is centralized fire stations.

I don't think the city put much thought, if any, about the lack of fire protection in the city's lower end, and that in my mind is nothing short of irresponsible at best.

The fire department that I knew and love is gone forever and that's a real shame. I'd like to think that there are a lot more guys still around that feel the same way. And I am sure there are.

EXAM TIME

The following questions are fictional questions that were really on the N.Y.S. Civil Service Exam for Fire Driver/Firefighter. Or at least they should have been.

These events are not fiction they really happened. (Exam answers on last page w/ explanations.)

1. If the pumper truck runs and drives just fine but the pump is not usable what would the best course of action to take be?

   A. Take it out of service until repairs are complete

   B. Take a picture of it.

   C. Send it out on false alarms only.

   D. Just say the hell with it and have another beer.

2. What is the best type of material to use when constructing a fire escape?

   A. Steel

   B. Scrambled Eggs

   C. Treated Lumber

   D. Chocolate Pudding

3. Please name the two most common types of fires. Please choose two.

   A. Big fires

   B. Car fires

   C. Little fires

   D. Bon fires

4. What is the best thing to do if you discover that birds have built a nest in the Aerial Ladder over the top of the cab?

   A. Feed it every morning.

   B. Call the National Audubon Society.

   C. Leave it there and drive the truck anyway in the Memorial Day Parade.

   D. Take it down; put it in the cab and save it for lunch.

5. While operating at the scene of a Brush Fire in the "Hollow Area" of the city, how would you respond to, as the Fire Driver/Operator of the apparatus, the fireman on the scene radios back to you asking to send down Indian Tanks?

   A. I am sorry there are no longer any Indian tanks on this pumper.

   B. What the hell are Indian tanks?

   C. Well ya better piss on it; the fire buffs took the Indian tanks off the truck.

   D. The hell with it let the damn hollow burn.

6. If you were on duty at a certain fire house, next to a certain bar in the lower end of the city, and a bar patron comes running into the firehouse saying that there is a fire next door, what is the best course of action?

   A. Pretend the incent never happened

   B. Go back to the driver's quarters and watch T.V.

   C. Walk next door to the bar to see for yourself what's going on without notifying the other companies of the incident.

   D. Or call on the fire phone and alert the other companies of the fire.

1. Answer to question number one is C. These words were actually spoken by then Fire Chief James East when the pump on pumper one was out of service. F.Y.I. He was dead serious.

2. Answer to question number two is C. The very treated lumber that was delivered to the Hills Firehouse one summer morning while I was on duty.

3. The correct answers to question number three are A and C. These words were repeatedly uttered by the Immortal Doug "The Bug" Cucumber many times over the years.

4. The answer to this question is also C. We discovered the birds nest built into the front of the Aerial Ladder as we were preparing to step off in the Memorial Day Parade. The fat little bastard of a driver on duty (we'll call him Newman) was too lazy to remove it so it rode the entire parade route. And yes there was a live sparrow living in it.

5. The answer to question number five is again C. These words were actually put out over the Pumper Four radio by fire driver Hank Really who never pulled any punches. He was later reprimanded by Chief East who was monitoring the call.

6. The answer to question number six is, yes C again (I like the letter C). This event really took place when a big shot driver (we'll call him Chuck) walked next door to the Tavern without notifying the other companies. End result total loss.

FIRE HOUSES

Truck No. 1 -   Jas. Hill Hook & Ladder Co.
                463-2883

Pumper No. 1 - Jas. N. Ring Co.
                449-7921

Pumper No. 2 - G.S. Mink & T. Claxton Hose Co.
                465-3243

Pumper No. 3 - E.F. Hart Hose Co.
                436-7794

Pumper No. 4 - Chemical & Hose Co.
                462-1864

HOSPITALS

Albany Medical Center 445-3125

Child's Hospital 462-4211

Memorial Hospital 471-3221

Veteran's Hospital 462-3311

St. Peter's Hospital 454-1550

*****

***

COMPLIMENTS OF—

JAMES HILL HOOK AND

LADDER CO. NO. 1

INCORPORATED IN 1892

NOW IN ITS 89TH YEAR

EMERGENCY FIRE PHONE..465-6853

SPECIAL BOX

333—GENERAL ALARM ASSEMBLY

FIRE ALARM NUMBERS

12	Third Ave. & Washington St.
13	Broadway at Boys Club
14	Herrick & Elm St.
15	Third Ave. near High St.
16	South St. & Aiken Ave.
17	St. John's Convent
18	Third Ave. & Adams St.
19	Fourth Ave. & East St.
21	Second Ave. & Green St.
23	Broadway & Fourth Ave.
24	Broadway & Third Ave.
25	Broadway & Second Ave.
26	Broadway & Columbia St.
27	City Hall—505 Broadway
31	Broadway & Aiken Ave.
32	Washington St. & First Ave.
34	South St. below Columbia St.
35	Moch Terr. & Aiken Ave.
36	Renwyck Place Apartments
41	South St. at Ashland Chemical
42	East St. & Second Ave.
43	Columbia St. & Aiken Ave.
45	South St. at City Line
51	Nelson Ave. & Belmore Pl.
52	River Road at Atlantic Oil Co.
53	River Road at Tidewater Oil Co.
54	General Anline
56	Winthrop
61	Willow Ridge Apartments
62	Summit & Dubuque St.
63	St. Joseph's School

71	Rensselaer Housing
72	Amtrak Turbo Bldg.
112	Fort Crailo School No. 1
113	Renss. Jr-Sr High School Entrance
115	Van Rensselaer Elementary School
122	Broadway & Harrison Ave.
123	Glen & Fourth St.
132	Partition & First St.
134	Albany Woolen Mills
142	Partition & Third St.
211	Broadway & Pine St.
223	First St. & Glen St.
224	Catherine & Third St.
231	Harrison Ave. between 2nd & 3rd St.
233	Harrison Ave. & Sixth St.
311	Broadway & Tracy St.
312	Central Ave. & Second St.
313	Van Rensselaer Heights Apartments
314	Willow & Lawrence St.
315	Washington Ave. & First St.
321	Broadway & McNaughton Ave.
322	Washington Ave. & Fourth St.
331	Fifth St. & Central Ave.
334	Barnetts Mill—Forbes Rd.
341	Second & Church St.
411	Elmhurst & Park Ave.
412	Anderson Pl. at Van Renss. Elem. School
413	Washington & Rockerfeller St.
421	Washington Ave. & Birchwood
422	Ash & Tenth St.
431	Highland Ave. & Lindbergh Ave.
512	Fowler Ave. & Third St.
511	Seventh & Chestnut
513	Washington Ave. at Monastery
516	Mann & Munger Ave.
621	Washington Ave. & Quay St.
623	Farley Drive

POLICE CALL

Police Headquarters.. 462-7451

AMBULANCE

Rensselaer Vol. Ambulance Serv.. 449-8777

Edwards Brothers Malloy
Oxnard, CA USA
January 9, 2014